The Kitten Girls are Scaredy Cats

Written by: Mickie Fosina

Illustrations: Susan Berger

To order additional copies of this book, contact:
Xlibris
1-888-795-4274
www.Xlibris.com
Orders@Xlibris.com

Dedication

To my wonderful grandchildren
I dedicate this book.
You have made my life so complete.
May you someday
have children of your own and
read to them the story of
the Kitten Girls.

Under the porch in the back of the house are seven little kittens and one little mouse.

The squeaky little mouse scared the kittens and they ran in all different directions.

Kitten Katt climbed up the side of the
house onto the windowsill where an apple pie
was cooling.

Looking very curious, she put one paw
into the pie. She licked her paw – it
tasted sooo good she went back for more.

Noticing kitten Katt enjoying the pie, the smallest kitten Jacqueline, climbed up to the window.

When putting her little paw into the pie she accidentally knocked it over --- off the windowsill.

OH, BOY, big trouble! The kittens
were on the run again....

Kitten Morgan, the spunkiest little kitten,
said "follow me!"

Then they all ran from the house to the garage
where a small opening in the door allowed them
to enter.

Snuggled together in the dark, they hoped
Mrs. Emerson wouldn't find them.
She would be sure to chase them with her
broom, as she always did! They were all sooo
afraid of the broom!

While huddled in the corner of the garage, and scared of being found, the kittens fell asleep...

During their nap the skies grew dark...

The sun disappeared and a very noisy thunderstorm with crackling thunder,
- streaks of lightening, and the pitter-patter of rain on the roof, scared the kittens even more.

Kitten Krissy, with her big blue eyes, told the kittens not to be afraid:

"The thunder and lighting are high in the sky and very soon the storm will pass by" and she started to sing:

"When the rain comes down and soaks
the ground, it helps to make the flowers grow.

When the sun comes out and clears the air
it makes us happy to see them there."

Kitten Amy, the only kitten with a yellow coat, peeked outside and saw the sun...

"OK, the storm is all gone and we can go out now".she said --- as she looked around to see if Mrs. Emerson was looking for them.

She wasn't around so they ventured out again.

Mrs. Emerson had gone to the store to buy more apples.

You see, the apple pie smelled sooo good that she decided to make another one!

While she was at the store buying apples, she saw packages of cat food and thought of the seven little kittens.

She said:

"Oh, those poor little kittens must be hungry to go into my apple pie, let me buy them some food".

As Mrs. Emerson was taking the groceries into the house she left the door open.

Guess what happened?

She turned around and the seven little kittens were in her kitchen!

She turned to them and said:

"What are you doing in my kitchen?"

and the kittens got scared and ran away...

Except two! Tori and Stephie, looking up at her said "meow, meow".

Mrs. Emerson leaned down, stroked the kittens and said "Are you hungry, would you like something to eat?"

She put two little bowls on the floor with food and the kittens started eating.

When the other little kittens realized that Tori and Stephie were not with them, they went back to the house.

They saw Mrs. Emerson sitting at the table
peeling apples and the kittens eating.

When she saw them, she said:
"So you've came back? Are you hungry too?"
She fed the rest of the kittens and
they realized she was now their friend.

After eating, the happy little kittens
went back to the park next to Mrs. Emerson's
house where they liked to play.

They weren't afraid of her anymore.
They weren't just little scaredy cats,
they were happy little kittens who had made
friends with Mrs. Emerson.

She was sooo happy with her new friends!
Since her boys, Matthew, Michael,
Chris and Timmy are off to school, the
kittens could now keep her company all day!

Printed in the United States
by Baker & Taylor Publisher Services

MICKIE FOSINA has been married to her husband Joe for over 50 years they have six married children five sons and one daughter all of which are both family and friends. She has been blessed with fifteen grandchildren who have inspired her to write her stories. She has been writing short stories and poems for about 20 years andhas now decided to publish her works.. Watch for three more of her stories coming soon, "The Kitten Girls Are Scaredy Cats", "The Trees Are Sleeping"and "Jacqueline's Magical Christmas" The Fosina's principally reside in New Rochelle, NY."

ISBN 978-1-4691-8172-1

Xlibris

Rocket Rangers

Man's Quest to fly like Buck Rogers

**Aerospace Heroes Commemorative
Vol. 2**

With vivid photo histories of the
Jetvest, Rocketbelt, Jetbelt, MMU, SPK and S.A.F.E.R

Edited by
Nelson Louis Olivo
Aerospace Historian